This book belongs to :

~~Oscar Paul~~

Gilbert

Original edition published in French under the title "Raymond le bison",
Les éditions la courte échelle, 2019. Copyright © Les éditions la courte échelle 2019.

Published in Canada and the United States in 2021 by Orca Book Publishers.
orcabook.com

Library and Archives Canada Cataloguing in Publication
Title: Raymond the buffalo / Lou Beauchesne ; illustrations, Kate Chappell ; translated by
Christelle Morelli and Susan Ouriou.
Other titles: Raymond le bison. English
Names: Beauchesne, Lou, 1978– author. | Chappell, Kate, illustrator. |
Morelli, Christelle, translator. | Ouriou, Susan, translator.
Description: Translation of: Raymond le bison.
Identifiers: Canadiana (print) 20200331345 | Canadiana (ebook) 20200331353 |
ISBN 9781459826175 (hardcover) | ISBN 9781459826182 (PDF) | ISBN 9781459826199 (EPUB)
Classification: LCC PS8603.E28 R3913 2021 | DDC jc843/.6—dc23

Library of Congress Control Number: 2020944959

Summary: In this transitional picture chapter book, a buffalo ends up
outside a child's favorite storybook and living in the local library.

Orca Book Publishers is committed to reducing the consumption
of nonrenewable resources in the making of our books. We make
every effort to use materials that support a sustainable future.

Orca Book Publishers gratefully acknowledges the support for its publishing
programs provided by the following agencies: the Government of Canada,
the Canada Council for the Arts and the Province of British Columbia
through the BC Arts Council and the Book Publishing Tax Credit.

We acknowledge the financial support of the Government of Canada through
the National Translation Program for Book Publishing, an initiative of the
*Roadmap for Canada Official Languages 2013-2018: Education,
Immigration, Communities,* for our translation activities.

Artwork created using gouache, pencil crayon and Photoshop.

Cover and interior artwork by Kate Chappell
Edited by Liz Kemp
Translated by Susan Ouriou and Christelle Morelli

Printed and bound in China.

24 23 22 21 • 1 2 3 4

Raymond the Buffalo

Lou
Beauchesne

illustrated by Kate
Chappell

translated by Susan Ouriou
and Christelle Morelli

ORCA BOOK PUBLISHERS

For Julie and all the characters who
are part of me. Thank you for existing.

Lou

Chapter One

Raymond was a buffalo. He was a very special buffalo, because he lived in the pages of a book. A book in which he was the hero.

Brave, strong and hairy, he faced danger while singing a happy song.

My name is Raymond, and I am a buffalo, and pickles with lemon is the food I adore. I sing this song to help my worries be gone. Pum, pum, pum, pum, pum, pum, pum, pum, pum, pum, pum.

The book belonged to Gilbert, a quiet boy who was also brave and strong but not the least bit hairy.

Despite their differences, Gilbert and Raymond were inseparable. Like the right butt cheek and the left butt cheek, they were always together.

Here they are in the park...

at the dentist...

in a restaurant...

and at the pool.

One day something huge happened that
shook up the lives of these two friends.
Gilbert met

a dinosaur.

From that moment on, it was all he could talk about. Dinosaur this, dinosaur that. He even dreamed about dinosaurs.

His mother was happy to see that her son had another interest. She took him to the library, where they found an entire collection of books about dinosaurs. Gilbert came home smiling from ear to ear, his arms loaded down with books.

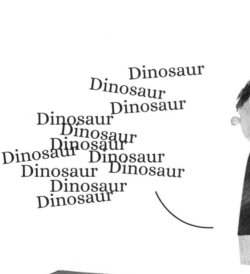

Dinosaur
Dinosaur
Dinosaur
Dinosaur
Dinosaur
Dinosaur
Dinosaur
Dinosaur
Dinosaur
Dinosaur
Dinosaur
Dinosaur

Raymond, on the other hand, felt abandoned. Dinosaurs had taken his place.

Chapter Two

One morning while Gilbert was at school, his mother noticed the pile of books on her son's nightstand. "Oh dear! I have to return these books to the library before they're overdue."

It's about time, thought Raymond.

I LOVE DINOSAURS

PREHISTORIC ANIMALS

THE LOVE OF A DINOSAUR

DINOSAURS FOR DUMMIES

ALL YOU NEED TO KNOW ABOUT DINOSAURS

THE BRONTOSAURUS ENCYCLOPEDIA

RAYMOND THE BUFFALO

DINOSAURS

IN THE TIME OF DINOSAURS

TYRANNOSAURUS AND ME

But because she was hurrying, Gilbert's mother accidentally picked up *Raymond the Buffalo* along with the dinosaur books!

Raymond left his home in a plain plastic bag. His heart was breaking. He was worried he'd never see Gilbert again.

On the way to the library,

he passed the neighbor's cat,

flew over dog poop

and sat next to a salami on the bus.

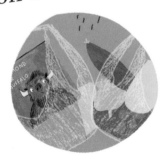

He thought about all the hikes he and Gilbert had gone on, and all the hikes he would never go on again.

When they walked into the library, Raymond gasped at the sheer size of the building. And all the books! He'd had no idea there could be so many books.

Raymond had never been in a library. Before belonging to Gilbert, he had belonged to Gilbert's father and grandfather. Before that? He had no idea, it was so long ago. Who knew? Maybe he had come from another planet.

The little buffalo was brought down to earth as soon as the woman behind the counter spoke to Gilbert's mother.

"Hello!
Books to return? Just throw them down the chute."

Raymond almost cried. He was made of paper, and he didn't know how to swim!

He was terrified! Raymond had battled the worst kinds of danger in his book— freezing cold, fierce dragons, torrential storms. But he didn't think he could survive a waterfall!

He did his best to sing.

M...my... n... name... is...
Ray... Ray... Raymond...

But he couldn't finish. The moment
he felt himself topple over the edge,
he fainted.

Chapter Three

When Raymond came to, he was surprised to notice that

1. He wasn't dead.
2. He wasn't even wet.
3. He was sitting at the bottom of a wooden box.

Even more surprising, he was sitting outside his book. Yes, really. Like a baby bird sitting beside its egg.

How had that even happened? He had no idea! However it had happened, he didn't want to stick around to figure it out. After all, wasn't he a brave buffalo?

Raymond grabbed his book as he got up. There was no way he was leaving it behind! They'd been through too many adventures together. On his way, he passed a couple of dinosaurs.

"Howdy, friends!"

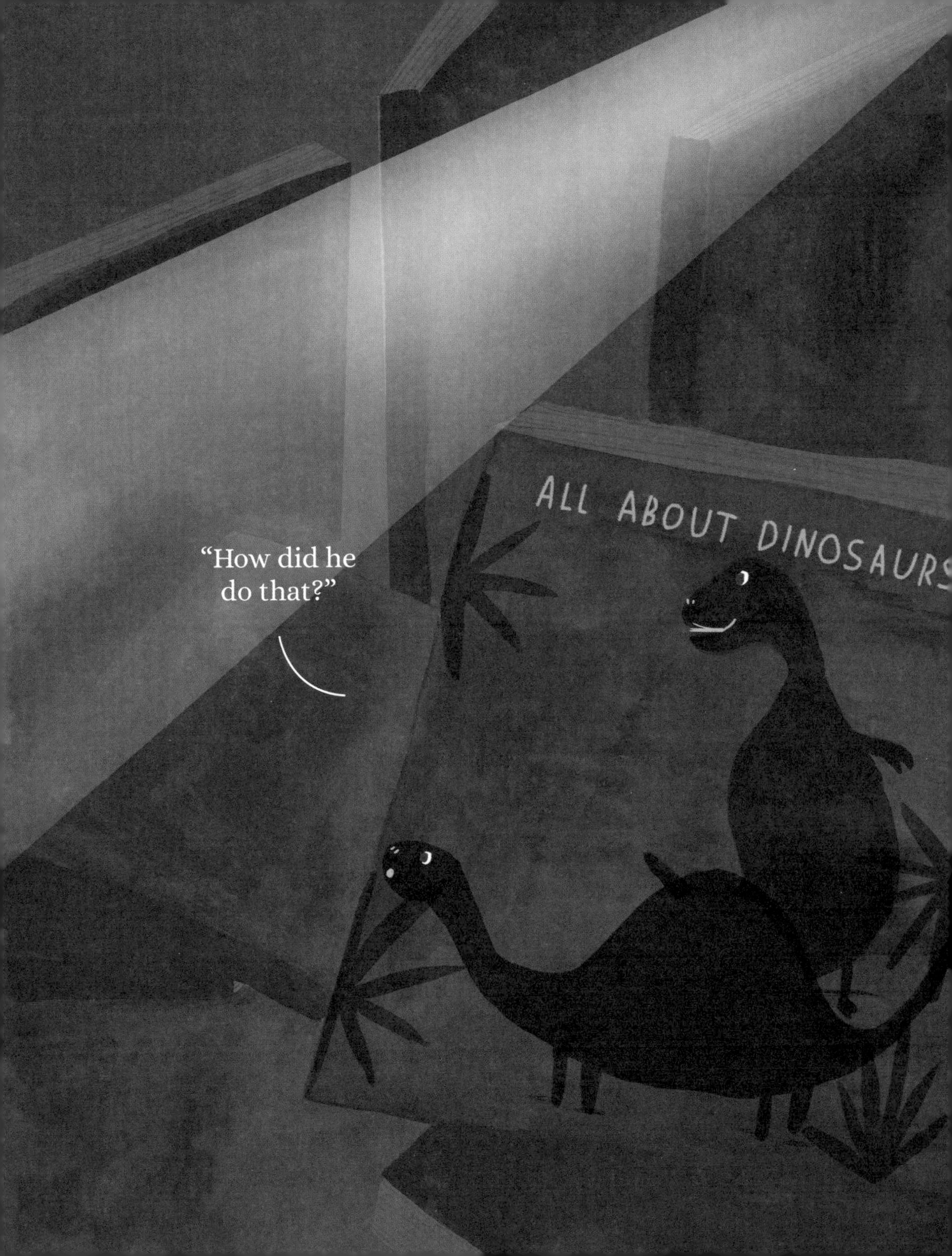

"How did he do that?"

When he reached the top, he peered outside the box. What he saw sent shivers down his spine. The librarian sat at her desk, armed with a pair of scissors, destroying a comic book. The poor book was in pieces.

Raymond knew he had to get out of this place as **fast as possible**.

There was a long drop between him and the floor. He backed up several steps. For an extra boost of courage, he sang his quiet song:

My name is Raymond,
and I am a buffalo,
and pickles with lemon
is the food I adore.
I sing this song
to help my worries be gone.
Pum, pum, pum, pum, pum,
pum, pum, pum, pum, pum, pum, pum.

And then, like a star athlete, he took a flying leap.

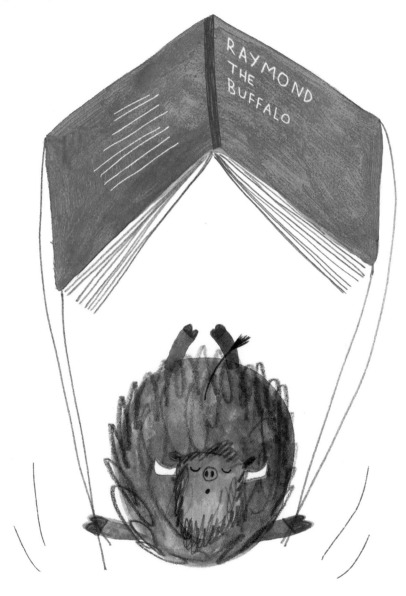

Chapter Four

A perfect landing! Once on firm ground he looked to the right and to the left. The path was clear. The only thing to do now was find the exit.

He moved forward slowly, cautiously, but then a herd of children appeared out of nowhere! Terrified that he was about to be trampled, he ran for an open door and threw himself through it.

Phew! A narrow escape! And by
pure luck it looked like he had stumbled
into a kitchen, where there was the
most wonderful thing! A huge jar full
of lemony pickles was sitting on
the table.

And because they were his greatest
weakness, Raymond couldn't resist
eating one…and then another. And one
more for the road. They were the best
he had ever tasted.

Meanwhile, Gilbert was starting to worry. When he got home from school, he realized that his *Raymond the Buffalo* book was missing. He had searched the house from bottom to top. His mother remembered her trip to the library—had she returned it by mistake?

They ran straight there.

Gilbert went directly to the circulation
desk and spoke to the librarian.

"Hello. I've lost my book, *Raymond
the Buffalo*. It's small, red and has a
beautiful picture on the cover. It's very
special to me. Have you seen it?"

The librarian carefully emptied the returns box, but *Raymond the Buffalo* was nowhere to be found. Gilbert was inconsolable. "We'll keep looking," his mother promised.

As for Raymond, his belly was full, and he'd dozed off next to the jar of pickles.

He was sleeping so soundly that he didn't hear footsteps approaching—**tap, tap, tap**—

or the door opening— **creeeeaaaak.** It was the librarian.

She was done for the day and had come into the kitchen to pick up her things before going home.

When Raymond and the librarian found themselves face-to-face, it was hard to tell who was more surprised.

"Who are you?"

"I'm Raymond the buffalo."

"The buffalo from the book? How about that!"

"A little boy with freckles, brown hair, a round little nose and sad eyes just came by. He's been looking for you everywhere."

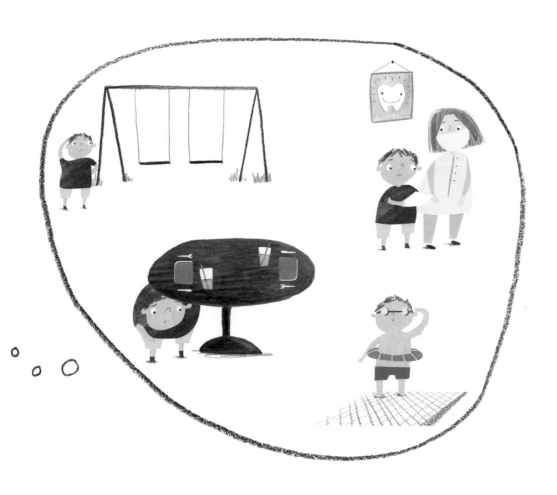

Raymond's heart started to race. It was Gilbert—his Gilbert! They would be reunited, and everything would go back to the way it had been. "Are you going to take me back home?" he asked the librarian.

She would have liked to, but she had no idea where he lived. She didn't even know his last name. Actually, Raymond didn't know his last name. He remembered taking the bus and that Gilbert's house was made of bricks and wasn't far from a park. That there was dog poop on the sidewalk, and the neighbor's cat was orange.

The librarian assured Raymond that Gilbert and his mother were bound to come back to the library. It was only a matter of time. "In the meantime, I'd offer you a pickle, little guy, but it looks like they're all gone."

It turned out that Nicole—that was the librarian's name—was really nice. And despite Raymond's first impression, she didn't destroy books. Just the opposite. She protected them, put them away carefully and cleaned them up. She even patched them sometimes, just the way a nurse would.

"You know, people aren't always careful. Some books come back with pages torn out or scribbled on," she explained.

Raymond felt like he could trust Nicole, and so he told her his story. He told her about Gilbert, the dinosaurs, his anger, his heartache, his arrival at the library, his fall down the chute, his fainting spell and his strange transformation.

The librarian listened quietly. When he was finished, she said, "You know, when something really upsetting happens in our lives, unusual things can happen."

Nicole offered to let Raymond stay at the library until Gilbert came back for him. However, he had to promise to behave and stay inside his book during opening hours, because animals were not allowed at the library. "Some people are allergic to anything out of the ordinary."

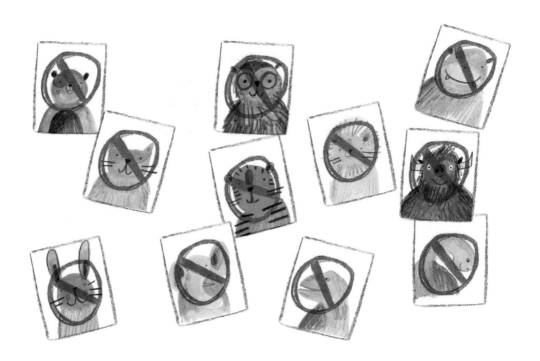

Chapter Five

There was a small glass cabinet at the front of the library that was used to showcase the various lost-and-found items Nicole had collected over the years. She placed Raymond the buffalo's book front and center.

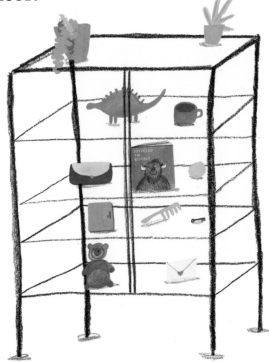

From his shelf the little buffalo had a clear view of the front door. For Raymond, this was the best view in the house, because it meant there was no way he would miss Gilbert coming in.

Raymond settled into a routine at the library. Before the doors opened every morning, he slid back inside his book in its place in the display case. As the day went on, he imagined his reunion with Gilbert. Every time a young boy walked through the front door, the little buffalo's heart sped up.

But it was never Gilbert.

In the evening, after the library had closed
for the day, Raymond and Nicole spent
time together. Their favorite thing to do
was to sit in the reading corner with a jar
of pickles between them. Then they'd bid
each other good night, and Nicole would
head home while Raymond got to work.

It turned out he had a talent for filing books. In particular, he had a knack for finding titles that had been mis-shelved by readers. Every book had a unique smell that Raymond could identify.

Nicole found this absolutely wonderful, since losing a book was one of her greatest fears. She would say, "Trying to find a lost book in a library is like looking for a grain of rice in a snowbank."

Nicole had a funny way of using words.

After several months of waiting at the library, Raymond finally got some news about Gilbert. He had moved away. At least, that's what the little girl who spotted the *Raymond the Buffalo* book in the display case said. She explained to Nicole that Gilbert used to be her neighbor. But no, she didn't know where he lived now. All she knew was that he had left with his family in a big yellow truck, looking sad and wearing a Montreal Canadiens jersey.

His favorite jersey, thought Raymond, his heart feeling heavy.

He stopped watching the front door.

"What's the point? Unless there's a miracle, I'll never see Gilbert again," he said to Nicole.

As cheerful as ever, she replied, "Don't tell me you don't believe in miracles!"

Chapter Six

As time passed, it worked its magic. Raymond never forgot about Gilbert, but he stopped being so sad about him. Raymond liked living at the library. He felt lucky to have met Nicole.

Here they are on Halloween,

at Christmas,

on Valentine's Day...

the best of friends.

Over time Nicole grew older, but Raymond didn't age one bit. Although the little buffalo tried to help around the library as much as he could, there came a time when Nicole decided she didn't want to spend her days working anymore. A new librarian would take her place.

On their last night together, Nicole and Raymond talked and cried a little as they ate lemony pickles. Nicole promised Raymond she would visit often, and Raymond promised to look after the books.

"But not tonight—I just don't have it in me," he said.

As Nicole left the library, she placed her friend in the lost-and-found case. Over the years, items had come and gone. Some had been claimed by their owners, while new items had been added.

"You mustn't lose hope," Nicole told Raymond. "You never know what the future holds."

Then she blew him a kiss. Raymond watched her walk away as he sang:

My name is Raymond,
and I am a buffalo,
and pickles with lemon
is the food I adore.
I sing this song
to help my worries be gone.
Pum, pum, pum, pum, pum,
pum, pum, pum, pum, pum, pum, pum.

The next morning the new librarian showed up for his first day at the library. The moment he laid eyes on *Raymond the Buffalo*, a tear ran down his cheek.

"Unbelievable! This is my book from when I was a boy. I've been looking for this..."

Raymond's heart melted. He couldn't believe his eyes. It was Gilbert. His Gilbert! He hadn't even recognized him now that he'd grown so hairy and tall!

Fortunately, the love between the two friends had not changed at all.

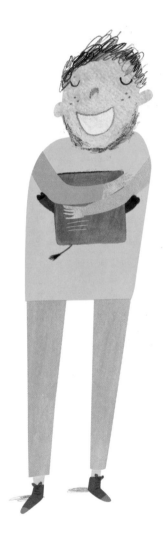

The end.

Lou Beauchesne is an author and illustrator of over twenty books for young readers including *La princesse cowboy* and *La guerre des suces*. She began writing and illustrating small books that she sold to her neighbors and has been writing ever since. Lou writes and draws from her home in Quebec.

Kate Chappell is a freelance illustrator living and working from her home in Lincolnshire, UK. She graduated from Falmouth University with a degree in illustration in 2013 and uses a mix of traditional textures and digital techniques to create fun, dynamic characters and illustrations. Kate has created art for Google, Stella Artois, Nespresso, Dove and many others and tries to include elements of humor in her work whenever possible.